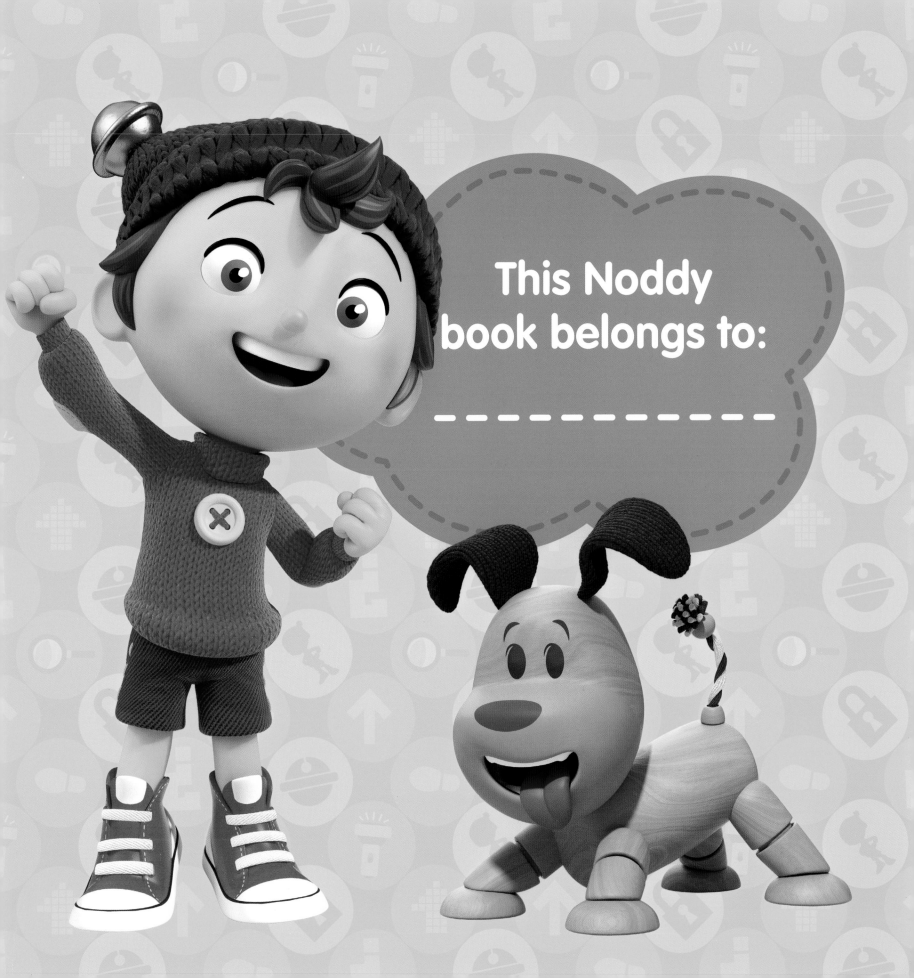

This Noddy
book belongs to:

_ _ _ _ _ _ _ _ _ _ _

Hodder Children's Books

First published in Great Britain in 2016 by Hodder and Stoughton
Noddy © 2016 DreamWorks Distribution Limited. All rights reserved.

The moral rights of the author and illustrator have been asserted.

A CIP catalogue record of this book is available from
the British Library.

ISBN 978 1 444 94096 1

10 9 8 7 6 5 4 3 2 1

Printed and bound in Slovakia

MIX
Paper from
responsible sources
FSC® C104740

Hodder Children's Books
An imprint of Hachette Children's Group
Part of Hodder and Stoughton
Carmelite House
50 Victoria Embankment
London EC4Y 0DZ

An Hachette UK Company
www.hachettechildrens.co.uk
www.hachette.co.uk

Noddy

Bumpy

The Pirates

Smartysaurus

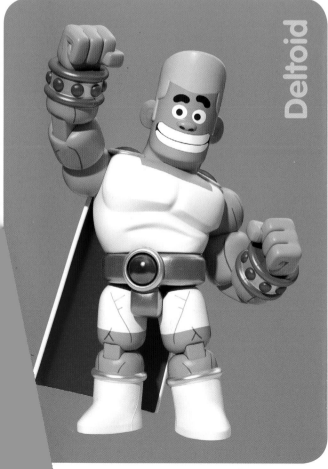

Deltoid

Bling

Fuse

Big Ears

Hoof

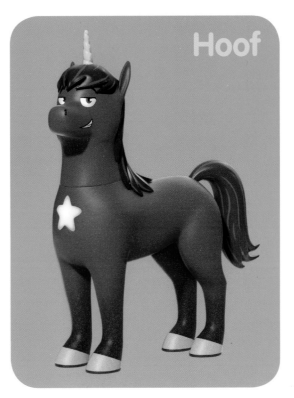

Queen Sparklewings

The Pockets

Pat-Pat

Revs

Cloppycorn

Hello, I'm
NODDY!

Did you know that I am a REAL DETECTIVE? If there's a mystery to solve, you can count on me!

First, I ring the bell on my hat. Ting-a-ling! Then I open up a brand new case. In Toyland, a mystery could happen anywhere . . .

underneath
a rainbow,

inside a
science lab

or even on
the deck of a
pirate ship!

I live in a little, round house in Toy Green. It's got a blue roof, a bell on the chimney and a slide to take me downstairs. **Whoosh!**

Someone very special lives with me. Can you guess who it is?

That's right! It's **BUMPY**.
Bumpy helps me with my detective work. Every time
he sniffs out a clue, his tail goes wag-wag-wag!

Detectives are super-busy. When I need to get somewhere fast, REVS is always ready. He's the best car in Toyland! Revs doesn't just zoom from here to there, he helps solve mysteries, too.

Today we're going to see my friend, Big Ears.
Would you like to come along? Toot! Toot! Jump in,
let's go!

Have you met **BIG EARS**? He's very old,
very wise and he lives in a toadstool house.

Here we are. Big Ears? BIG EARS? Where are you?

Oh no! Big Ears has gone!
I need to open a new case.

Who? What? When?
Where? Why? How?
Let's investigate now.

Let's call this,
'THE CASE OF MISSING
BIG EARS'.

Let's look for clues. We'll start with my best friend **PAT-PAT**. She lives in a treehouse with the three Pockets.
I wonder if they have seen Big Ears?

Pat-Pat is secretly drawing something. It looks like a book! Quick as a flash, she hides it away.

Let's try somewhere new. Revs turns towards Brick-a-Build. Good idea! Maybe **FUSE** can give us a clue?

Fuse is a robot. He's brilliant at inventing things… and remembering stuff, too! Let's tell him all about the case of Missing Big Ears.

Uh-oh. Fuse hasn't got time to talk. He's too busy in his workshop to help a detective today! He's just finished building a special tool.

Now I have a job to do AND a case to solve!
Let's go! We drive all the way over
to Animal Acres.
SMARTYSAURUS
is waiting inside her Dinolab.

Smartysaurus is very pleased.
She fits the tool into a machine,
then turns a key on the side.

What a lovely song. Smartysaurus'
machine is a music player!

Thank you, Noddy! Will you stay and dance with me?

LA! LA! LA!

There's no time for dancing – we've got a mystery
to solve. Maybe my friend Deltoid can help? Let's
go and see.

DELTOID is an action toy with a big heart and even bigger muscles.
Oh my! It looks like he's dancing, too!

I've got to practise my moves. Oops! Please don't join in – it's a secret!

Deltoid shakes his arms and kicks his legs.
He hasn't seen Big Ears either.

Deltoid dances up to his house,
leaps inside and shuts the door.

Where has Big Ears gone?

Being a detective can be tough, but I have a special gadget to help me. Let's get out my Who-What-Where Book!

A map of Toyland pops up. Look! We haven't been to the Fairy Castle yet.
Toot! Toot! We're on our way!

The Fairy Castle is a magical place. Look! There's Queen **SPARKLEWINGS**. The Queen is playing hide-and-seek in the Royal Maze.

Oh Noddy! I can't talk now. I'm trying to find the Fairies.

Queen Sparklewings disappears. **Ting!**

No Queen Sparklewings. No Fairies. And still no Big Ears!

Noddy the Toyland Detective never gives up. Let's explore somewhere new. The pirates live in Daredale. Ahoy there! Can you see their ship?

There are the **PIRATES**!
But what are they doing with all
those balloons?

Nothing to
see here, shipmate.
On your way!

There aren't many places left to try. Even the **NAUGHTICORNS** are too busy to help our hunt for Big Ears.

Bling, Cloppycorn and Hoof swish their tails. They are getting ready for something special.

A book, a music player, a dance, some balloons and a hide-and-seek game, but still no Big Ears! What a mystery.

It is getting late. Oh dear! What should a detective do now?

Woof! Woof!

I know, Bumpy. I wish I could ask Big Ears, too. Let's go home. Maybe we've missed a clue along the way.

The sky is dark. The stars are shining. It's time for Bumpy to curl up in his kennel.

SURPRISE! Here's Big Ears, Pat-Pat and all of my Toyland friends!

Three cheers for Noddy!

That's the mystery – Big Ears has organised a surprise party.

Pat-Pat has made a special book full of lovely photos. There's music, games and lots and lots of dancing.

Can you dance along? Put one hand on your hip, the other in front then point your finger to the sky!

The mystery is solved. We found Big Ears AND had the best party ever. Good job, everyone!

CASE CLOSED!